For Tom
from
Aunt Nan and Uncle Jerry
Christmas 1968

# THE TIGER IN THE TEAPOT

STORY BY BETTY YURDIN

# THE
# TIGER IN THE TEAPOT

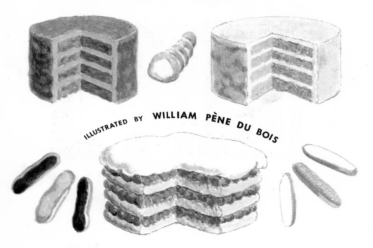

ILLUSTRATED BY WILLIAM PÈNE DU BOIS

HOLT, RINEHART AND WINSTON · NEW YORK  CHICAGO  SAN FRANCISCO

*T*here was once a family who owned a most tremendous teapot. It was one of the biggest teapots you ever saw.

One afternoon Mama set out the good things for tea. Chocolate cake, sponge cake, spice cake, vanilla cake, walnut cake, strawberry shortcake, and cookies. Mama set a kettle of water on to boil and took the teapot down from the shelf.

But when she took the cover off
the teapot, what do you think she
saw inside?

A tiger!

"Tiger," said Mama, who was in a hurry, "I must ask you to get out of there right away. I have to make the tea."

But the tiger wouldn't get out.

So Mama called Big Sister Susie, who was busy slicing up the chocolate cake.

"Susie," she said, "please come here and help me get this tiger out of our teapot."

Susie was very firm. "That's no place to be at teatime," she told the tiger. "You know that as well as I do. It's teatime and we need that teapot. Hop out now!"

8

But the tiger didn't even move.

Right then, Great Aunt Josephina came to the kitchen to help carry the chocolate cake. "Gracious me," she said, "this won't do at all."

"When I was a girl," Great Aunt Josephina said to the tiger, "tigers were much more polite. Whenever they were told to get out of a teapot, they always got right out."

But the tiger wouldn't get out of the teapot, no matter what Great Aunt Josephina said.

"Here come the Twins," said Mama. "They'll scare the tiger out of there."

"Get out of that teapot fast, you tiger," said One Twin, "or I'll thump you on the head with my cricket bat."

"And when he's finished," said the Other Twin, "I'll thump you some more."

The Twins talked that way because they liked everybody to think they were fierce. They really didn't ever thump anybody on the head.

Still, the tiger didn't know that.

12

But even so, the Twins couldn't make the tiger get out of the teapot.

Now it was past regular teatime. The Three Middle Boys came in from the sitting room. Papa had sent them to find out why the tea was late.

"Oh, we'll get the tiger out," said the Three Middle Boys. "It won't take a minute."

"Listen, Tiger," the Three Middle Boys said, "you have no idea how angry Papa can be when his tea is late. If you don't get out of there immediately, you're sure to be sorry."

14

But the tiger didn't seem to worry about upsetting Papa, and he just wouldn't get out of the teapot.

The door opened and Middle Sister Jane came into the kitchen. Papa had got tired of waiting. He had sent her to find out why the Three Middle Boys didn't come back and tell him why the tea was late.

"I know what to do," said Middle Sister Jane. "Look here," she said to the tiger, "just get out for awhile and let us use the teapot to make our tea. After we've finished you can climb right back in, if you like."

But the tiger wouldn't get out of the teapot, not even for awhile.

By now the tea was very late and getting later and later. When the door opened this time it was Papa himself who came into the kitchen.

"We'll just see about this!" Papa said to the tiger, and he was very angry. "I don't allow anybody to sit in my teapot when I want my tea."

The tiger sat very quietly in the teapot.

"There are laws about sitting in teapots when people want to use them," Papa thundered, and his face got bright red. "I'll call a policeman, and he'll make you get out."

The tiger was very quiet there inside the teapot.

"If you won't get out for the policeman, I'll call the Fire Department," Papa shouted. "They'll come at top speed with their sirens screaming. All the firemen will jump off the engines and drag the big hoses in here. Then I think you'll get out of our teapot, quick enough!"

20

The tiger looked straight at Papa, who was so upset, but stayed right where he was in the teapot.

Just then Littlest Sister Josie came home from a party. She was looking very pretty in her little white hat with three red cherries on top. There was no one at all in the sitting room when she went through. Nobody was in the dining room either. But when she came to the kitchen she found the entire family all there together.

"How nice to see everybody!" said Littlest Sister Josie. "And what a lovely tiger we've got in our teapot!"

22

Josie went over to the tiger and
patted him on the top of his head.
"Tiger," she asked him, "are you

quite comfortable in there? Are you sure it isn't cramping your tail? It's such a long, lovely tail."

"You're welcome to stay as long as you like, of course." Josie smiled at the tiger. "But wouldn't you rather come out and have some tea with us?

We would be pleased if you would."

"Why, yes. I'd like to do that. Thank you very much," said the tiger politely.

29

# And he did.

Betty Yurdin was born in Wisconsin and attended Montana State College. Although her stories have appeared in children's magazines, *The Tiger in the Teapot* is her first book to be published. The mother of two children, Mrs. Yurdin has lived in Europe since 1961 and now makes her home in Denmark.

William Pène du Bois, the celebrated author and illustrator of many fine children's books, was honored with the 1948 Newbery Medal for *The Twenty-One Balloons* and New York *Herald Tribune* Spring Book Festival Awards for *The Twenty-One Balloons* and *Lion*. Mr. Pène du Bois now lives in New York City with his wife, Willa Kim, the well-known stage designer.

About the Book: The text type is Palatino; the display type is Futura with hand lettering (on tiger skin binding); the book was printed by offset. William Pène du Bois illustrated the book in ink and water-color.